Meet the Author-Illustrator

Bernard Most likes his characters to find interesting ways to solve problems. In The Very Boastful Kangaroo, the teeny, tiny kangaroo finds a smart way to win the jumping contest. The author-illustrator wants his readers to know that even though they are small, they can do anything they want if they just try. Mr. Most always tells children to follow their dreams and to "never give up!"

Walt Chrynwski

Bernard Most

Look for these other Green Light Readers—
all affordably priced in paperback!

Level 1/Kindergarten–Grade 1

Big Brown Bear
David McPhail

Cloudy Day/Sunny Day
Donald Crews

Down on the Farm
Rita Lascaro

Popcorn
Alex Moran
Illustrated by Betsy Everitt

Sometimes
Keith Baker

What I See
Holly Keller

Level 2/Grades 1–2

A Bed Full of Cats
Holly Keller

Catch Me If You Can!
Bernard Most

The Chick That Wouldn't Hatch
Claire Daniel
Illustrated by Lisa Campbell Ernst

The Fox and the Stork
Gerald McDermott

I Wonder
Tana Hoban

Shoe Town
Janet Stevens and Susan Stevens Crummel
Illustrated by Janet Stevens

Green Light Readers is a trademark of Harcourt Brace & Company.

Green Light Readers
For the new reader who's ready to GO!

The Very
Boastful
Kangaroo

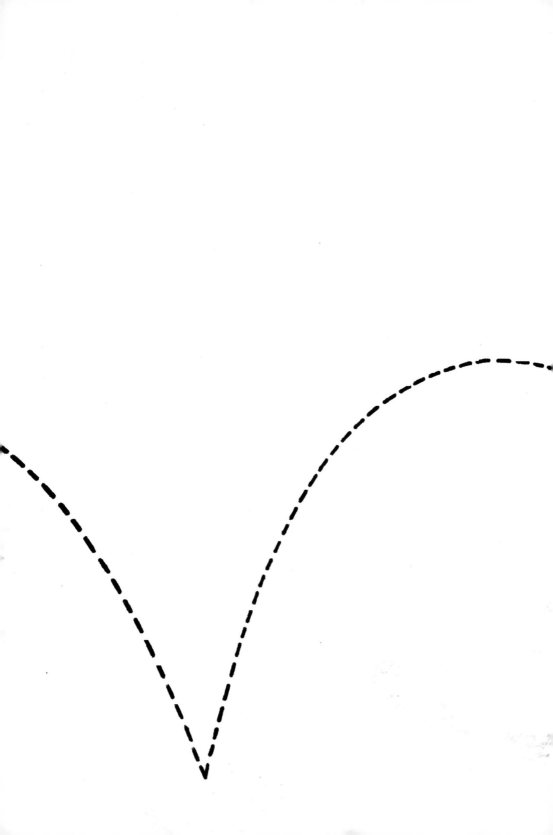

The Very Boastful Kangaroo

Bernard Most

Green Light Readers
Harcourt Brace & Company
San Diego   New York   London

First Green Light Readers edition 1999
Green Light Readers is a trademark of Harcourt Brace & Company.

Library of Congress Cataloging-in-Publication Data
Most, Bernard.
The very boastful kangaroo/Bernard Most.
p. cm.—(Green Light Readers)
Summary: A very, very boastful kangaroo brags that it can jump higher than
anyone, but a teeny, tiny kangaroo cleverly wins the jumping contest.
ISBN 0-15-202349-6
ISBN 0-15-202266-X pb
[1. Kangaroos—Fiction. 2. Contests—Fiction.] I. Title. II. Series.
PZ7.M8544Ve 1999
[E]—dc21 98-55234

A C E F D B

This story is about a very, very
boastful kangaroo.
"I can jump so, so high!" he bragged.
"No one can jump higher than I can!"

Just then a little kangaroo jumped up. "Let's have a jumping contest," she said. "Can you jump higher than these kangaroos can?"

"Oh yes," said the very, very boastful kangaroo. "I can jump much, much higher than any kangaroo! I'll win the contest because I'm the best!"

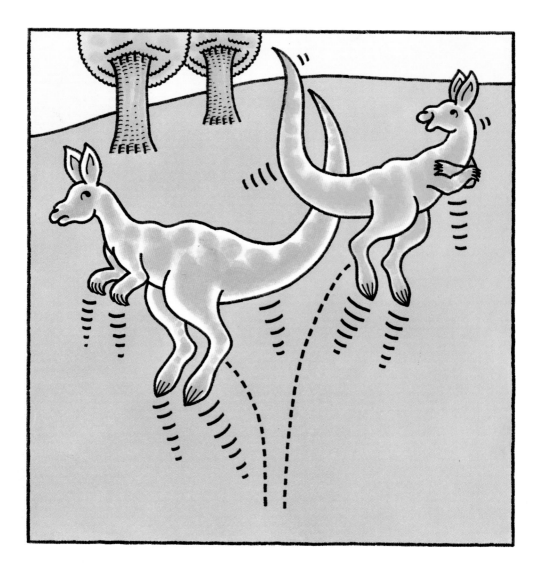

The first kangaroo jumped high. The very, very boastful kangaroo jumped even higher.

"See?" bragged the very, very boastful kangaroo. "I can jump higher. I'm the best!"

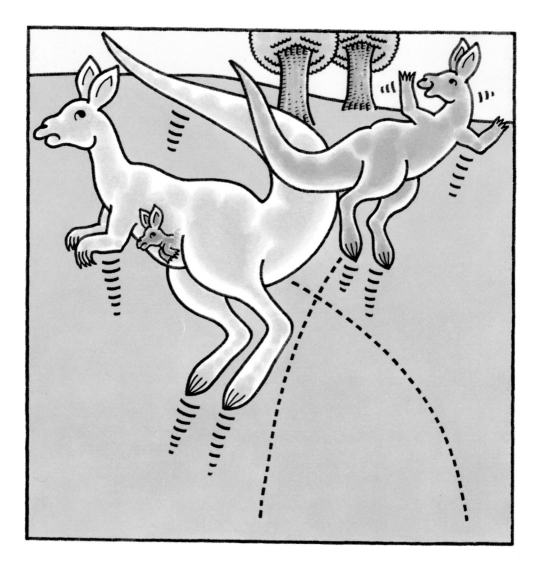

The next kangaroo jumped very high.
Even so, the very, very boastful
kangaroo jumped much higher.

"See?" the very, very boastful kangaroo bragged. "I win! I win the jumping contest."

"Not yet!" yelled a teeny, tiny kangaroo. "Can you jump higher than that tall tree?"

"That tree is much, much too tall!" said the very, very boastful kangaroo. "Even I can't jump higher than that tree!"

"If I jump higher than that tree, do I win the contest?" asked the teeny, tiny kangaroo.

The very, very boastful kangaroo
giggled. "Yes, but you're not going to
do it."

The teeny, tiny kangaroo jumped a teeny, tiny jump. Then she shouted, "I win! I win the contest … BECAUSE TREES CAN'T JUMP!"

All the kangaroos giggled and giggled—even the very, very boastful kangaroo!

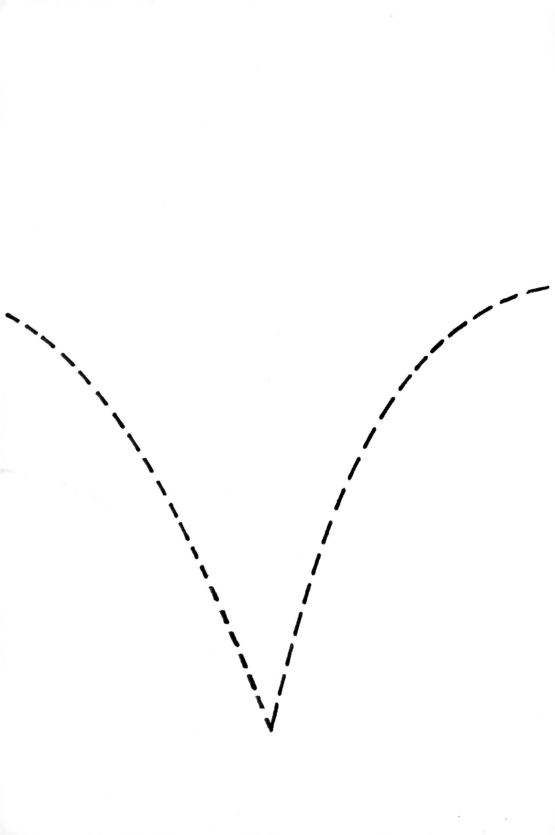

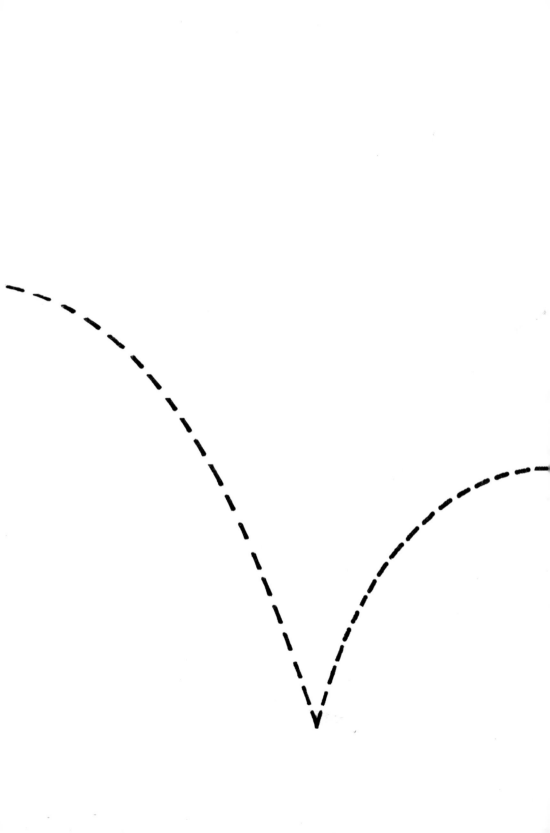

Display type set in Heatwave
Text set in Minion
Color separations by Bright Arts Ltd., Hong Kong
Printed by South China Printing Company, Ltd., Hong Kong
This book was printed on 140-gsm matte art paper.
Production supervision by Stanley Redfern and Ginger Boyer
Designed by Barry Age